The Little Book of Big Feelings

Christmas Adventure

As a way of saying thanks for your purchase, I'm offering a coloring book for FREE to my readers.

To get instant access just scan QR code
or go to:

www.booksbyluna.com

The Little Book of Big Feelings

The
Little Book
of Big Feelings

BELONGS TO

Christmas Adventure

Excitement's Sparkle

Theo's eyes are bright tonight,
Christmas Eve feels just right!
"Santa's coming!" he shouts with cheer,
Bunny smiles, "He's almost here!"
They hang socks by the fire,
And set out treats they all admire.
Theo snuggles into bed,
Dreams of Santa in his head.
Feeling excited is fun and bright,
It makes the season warm and light

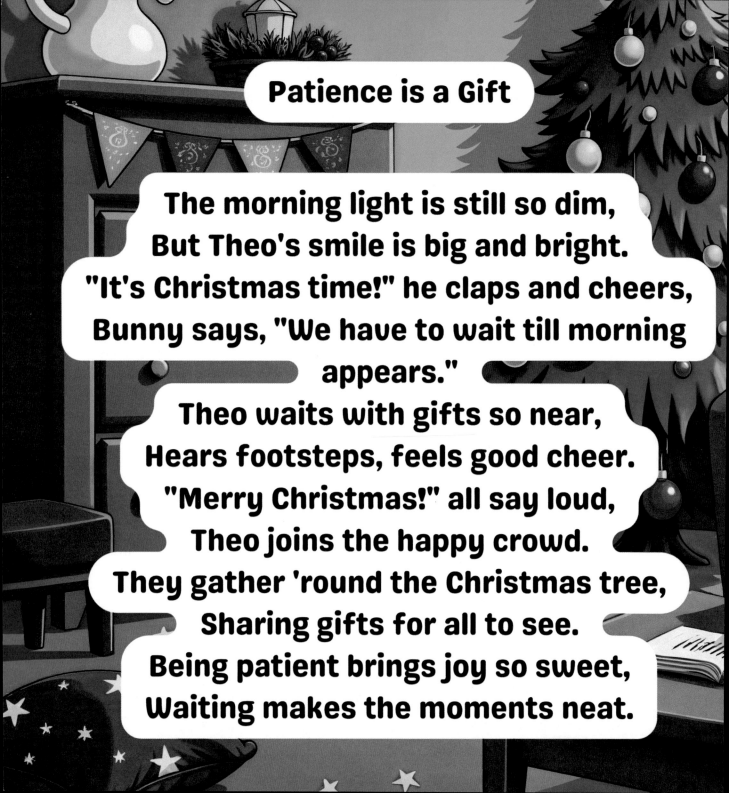

Patience is a Gift

The morning light is still so dim,
But Theo's smile is big and bright.
"It's Christmas time!" he claps and cheers,
Bunny says, "We have to wait till morning
appears."
Theo waits with gifts so near,
Hears footsteps, feels good cheer.
"Merry Christmas!" all say loud,
Theo joins the happy crowd.
They gather 'round the Christmas tree,
Sharing gifts for all to see.
Being patient brings joy so sweet,
Waiting makes the moments neat.

Disappointment's Surprise

No robot toy under the tree,
Theo frowns, "Oh dear me."
But look! An art set catches his eye,
Now he can draw robots, oh my!
With crayons, paper, and his imagination,
He creates a robot sensation.
If plans change, that's okay,
We can find new fun and play.

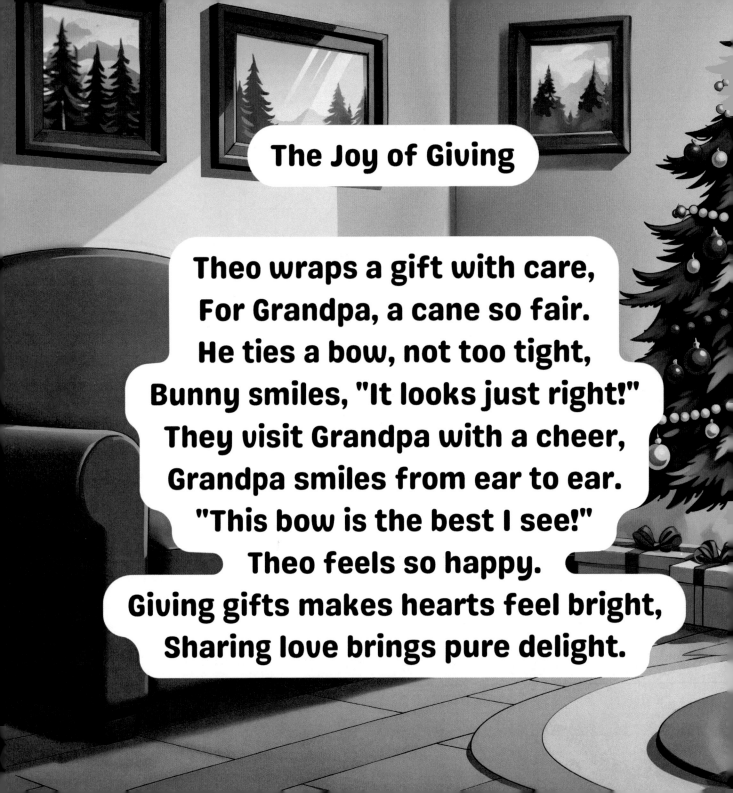

The Joy of Giving

Theo wraps a gift with care,
For Grandpa, a cane so fair.
He ties a bow, not too tight,
Bunny smiles, "It looks just right!"
They visit Grandpa with a cheer,
Grandpa smiles from ear to ear.
"This bow is the best I see!"
Theo feels so happy.
Giving gifts makes hearts feel bright,
Sharing love brings pure delight.

Gratitude's Flavor

"Yucky veggies," Theo says,
But Bunny has fun ways.
"Let's thank each food we eat,
It makes them yummy treats!"
"Thank you, carrot, big and bright,
Thank you, peas, so small and white."
Theo munches with a grin,
Grateful for each bite within.
Saying thank you makes meals fun,
Being grateful is for everyone.

Wonder's Twinkling Lights

Outside they go at night,
Christmas lights so bright.
Theo gasps, "Wow, so bright!"
Everything feels just right.
A snowman waves hello,
Candy houses all aglow.
Theo's eyes sparkle with delight,
Magic shines in every light.
Seeing wonders fills us with cheer,
Magic moments we hold dear.

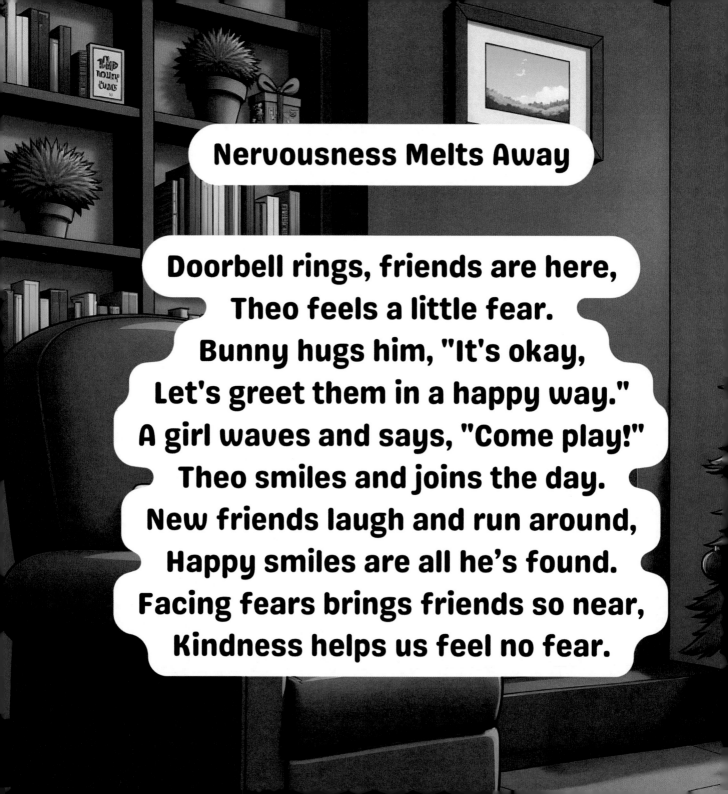

Nervousness Melts Away

Doorbell rings, friends are here,
Theo feels a little fear.
Bunny hugs him, "It's okay,
Let's greet them in a happy way."
A girl waves and says, "Come play!"
Theo smiles and joins the day.
New friends laugh and run around,
Happy smiles are all he's found.
Facing fears brings friends so near,
Kindness helps us feel no fear.

Finding Calm in Chaos

The house is noisy, full of cheer,
For Theo, it's a bit too near.
With Bunny, he finds a quiet spot,
Breathing slow helps quite a lot.
They count to ten, nice and slow,
Theo feels his worries go.
In the calm, he finds his way,
Ready to rejoin holiday play.
When it's loud, take a deep breath,
Calmness helps us feel our best.

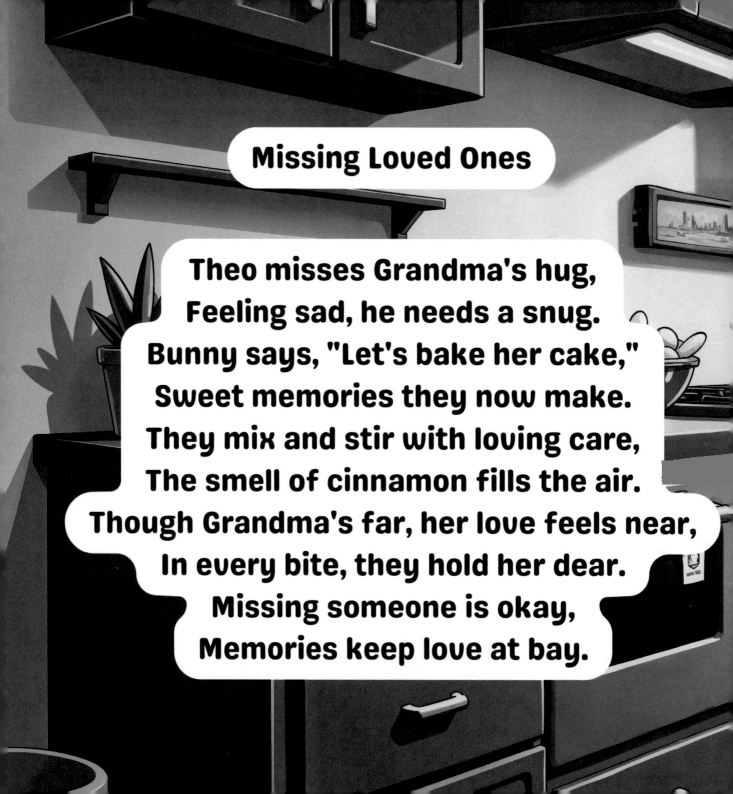

Missing Loved Ones

Theo misses Grandma's hug,
Feeling sad, he needs a snug.
Bunny says, "Let's bake her cake,"
Sweet memories they now make.
They mix and stir with loving care,
The smell of cinnamon fills the air.
Though Grandma's far, her love feels near,
In every bite, they hold her dear.
Missing someone is okay,
Memories keep love at bay.

Joy to the World

Theo sings a happy song,
"Joy to the World" all day long.
He dances 'round the Christmas tree,
Full of joy and happy glee!
Bunny hops and joins the fun,
They laugh and play with everyone.
Laughter fills the cozy room,
Chasing away any gloom.
Sharing joy makes hearts feel light,
Laughter turns our day so bright.

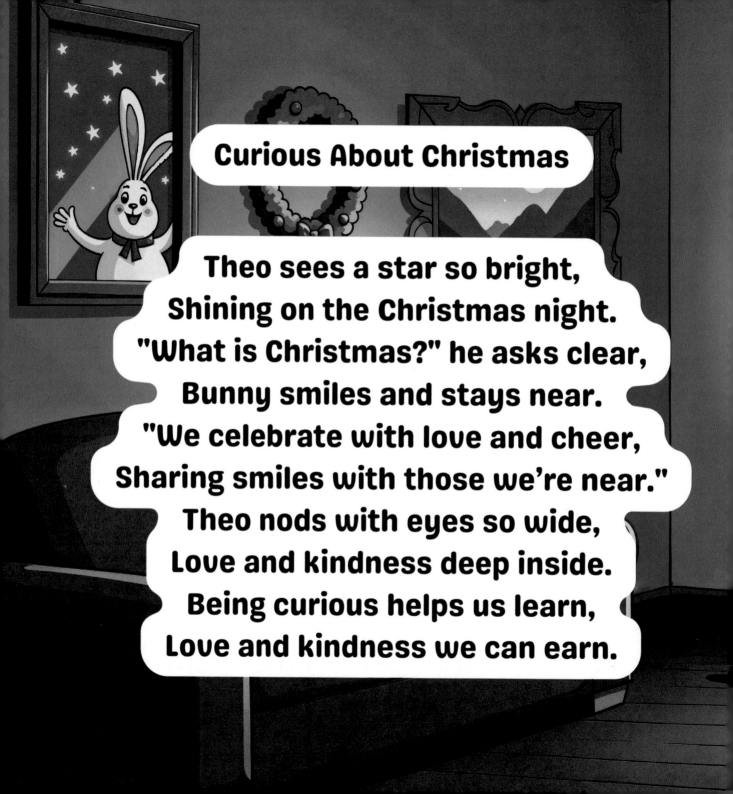

Curious About Christmas

Theo sees a star so bright,
Shining on the Christmas night.
"What is Christmas?" he asks clear,
Bunny smiles and stays near.
"We celebrate with love and cheer,
Sharing smiles with those we're near."
Theo nods with eyes so wide,
Love and kindness deep inside.
Being curious helps us learn,
Love and kindness we can earn.

Cozy Contentment

Fire crackles, soft and warm,
Snowflakes dance in every form.
Theo and Bunny snuggle tight,
Feeling cozy through the night.
Lights on the tree twinkle bright,
Theo yawns, it's time for night.
Theo dreams of things so sweet,
Happy hearts and sleepy eyes.
Feeling cozy brings us peace,
Warmth and love will never cease.

My Christmas Feelings

Draw or write about your favorite part of the story!

Thank You

Thank you so much for choosing "The Small Book of Big Feelings."
I know there are so many wonderful books out there, and I'm truly honored that you picked mine.
It means the world to me that you've taken this journey with me and my characters,
and I hope the story has touched your heart as much as it did mine while creating it.

Before you go, I have a small favor to ask. If you enjoyed the book, would you kindly consider leaving a review on the platform? Sharing your thoughts is the best way to support authors like me, and it helps others discover the magic of stories that nurture young minds.

Your feedback is so valuable—it helps me continue crafting books that inspire and support little readers like yours. I'd love to hear from you, and it would mean everything to know how the story resonated with you and your family.

Thank you again for being part of this adventure! Your support and feedback mean the world to me.

With heartfelt thanks,
Luna Rinne

Made in the USA
Las Vegas, NV
02 December 2024

13175020R00024